Parent's Guide

Holding the Pencil

Encourage your child to hold the pencil properly. The child should hold the pencil gently in between the thumb and the forefinger, about 1 or 2 cm above the tip.

The pencil should rest on the middle finger for proper support. This gentle grip allows the child to move the pencil easily for smooth writing movements.

Left hand

This book will help you to observe which hand the child favors. If your child is left-handed, tilt the page at a clockwise angle so that the top left corner is slightly higher than the right. Place the paper slightly to the left of the child's body to prevent smudging of letters.

Right hand

Keep your hand relaxed.

Bend your fingers, not your arm.

Don't press the pen too hard.

Practice

The handwriting of your child will improve if you encourage them to practice their motor skills constantly. You can encourage them to write on the sand, color the letters or cut letters with safety scissors.

ONE

Trace the number

TWO

Trace the number

1

2

3 →

Three

Trace the number

Four

Trace the number

Five

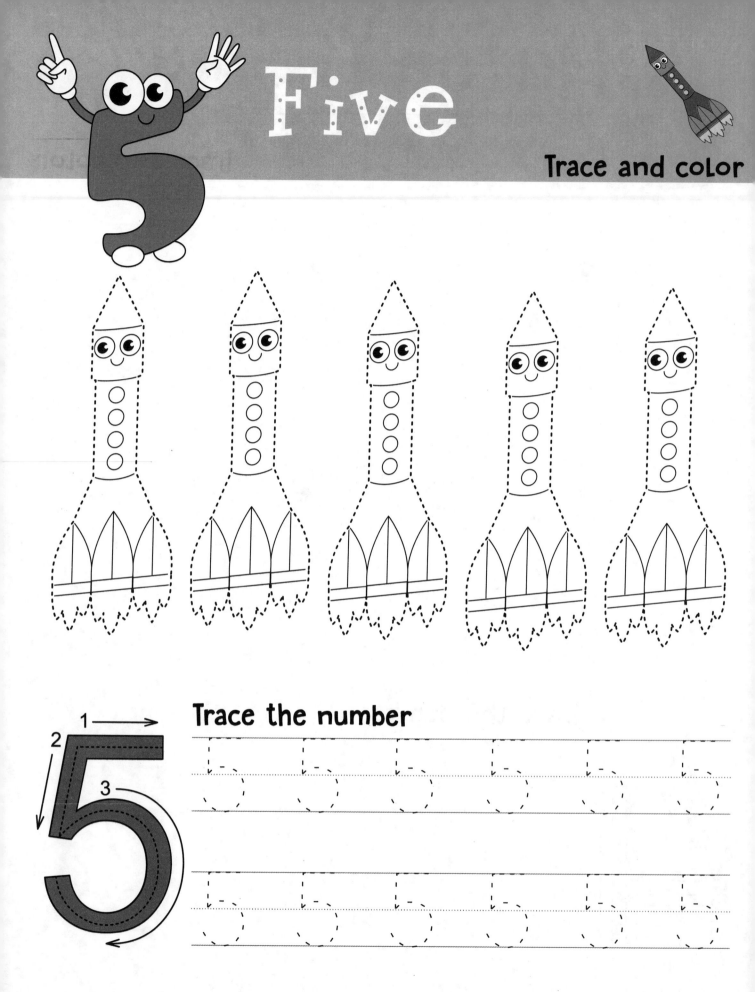

Trace the number

Match Them!

Trace the number and match with the correct group of items.

Six

Trace the number

Seven

Trace and color

Trace the number

Eight

Trace and color

Trace the number

Nine

Trace the number

Ten

Trace the number

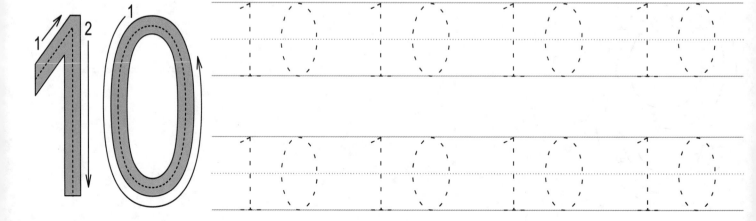

Match Them!

Trace the number and match with the correct group of items.

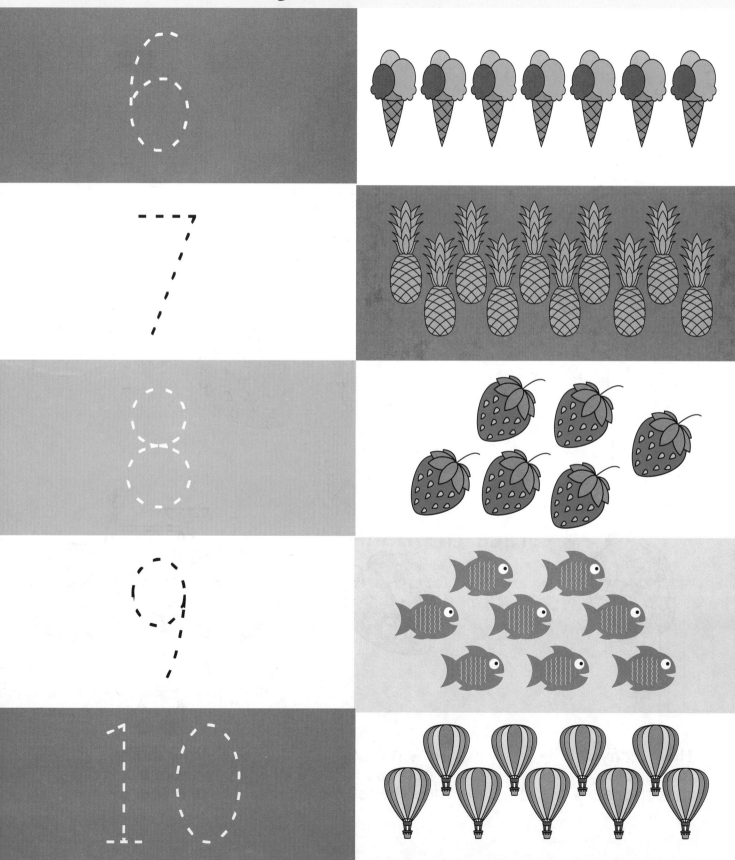

Colorful Counting

Count each different object. Then write your answer in the boxes below.

 How many
pineapples
are there?

 How many
bunnies
are there?

 How many
cars
are there?

TIP You can circle each type of object with a different color to keep track of your count.

 How many gift boxes are there?

 How many cycles are there?

 How many strawberries are there?

Write the Missing Numbers!